# Can You See Me Now?

The adventures of Mya Rebecca,
the little black pitbull.

This story is dedicated
to the rescues
who never turn away
from a dog
because he cannot
see or hear,
is lame or sick,
is a certain breed,
size or color
... and to the humans
who open their
hearts and homes and
love and care for them forever.

We thank you.

All proceeds from the sale of this book will benefit Rebound Hounds, a 501c3 organization
dedicated to the rescue, rehabilitation and rehoming of homeless animals.

On a cold winter morning, a little black pit bull puppy named Mya Rebecca was born in a raggedy cardboard box in the back of a large brownstone somewhere in Brooklyn, New York.

Her mother did her best to keep her babies warm and fed. She nursed till she had no milk left, licked them with her warm, soft tongue, and never let them out of her sight.

The man who sometimes came to feed Mya's mom, began to bring other humans into the backyard. Her mom would cry whenever they picked up one of her babies, as if she knew what was happening ...

For one by one, the humans took Mya Rebecca's brothers and sisters. Till only Mya Rebecca was left.

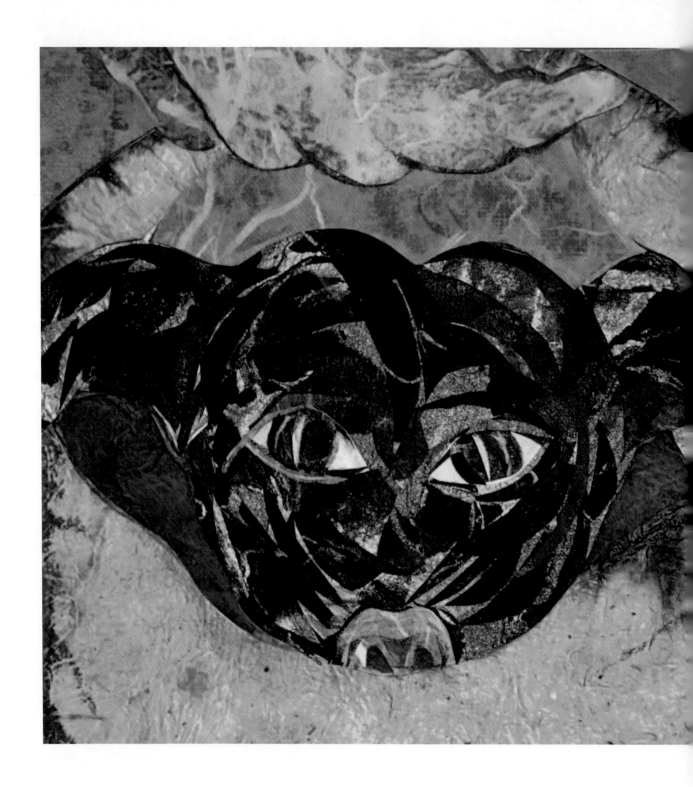

One morning the man came and picked Mya Rebecca up by the scruff of the neck and put her in a satchel. He roped her mom and dragged her to a shed he used for tools.

Mya's mom looked back at her daughter, her eyes large and afraid and very sad. Then she let out one long, piercing howl before she disappeared behind the door.

The man drove for a long time until they arrived at a large building. Inside was noisy and scary, dogs barking everywhere.

The man handed Mya Rebecca over to a nice lady with kind eyes who asked if she was his dog.

"Nope. She's a stray."

The woman sighed and shook her head as the man signed something and hurried out.

"Good luck adopting *her* out!" He said over his shoulder.

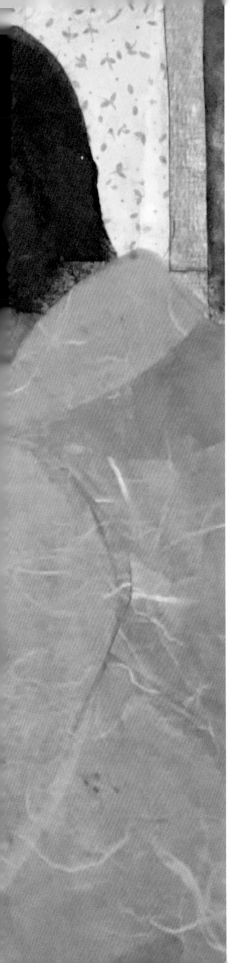

Mya Rebecca didn't like the scary place. She was put on a cold table. Her mouth was opened. She was poked at and stung.

Then she was taken to a room with lots of cages and dogs that barked when she entered. She crawled into the back corner of her cage, her tiny body shaking with fear.

The humans walked in and out all day long. They looked at the dogs, stuck their fingers in to pet them. Fed them treats. If they left with a dog, Mya knew it was something good, and she wanted that more than anything, to be noticed. To be taken home.

Day after day, Mya Rebecca waited. She jumped whenever a person walked down the aisle. She yipped a little and wagged her tail extra hard. Some stopped, looked, but then they moved on. No one took her out. No one took her home.

*It's like they don't even see me,* Mya thought. *It's like I'm invisible.*

In the yard Mya met a very old dog. His fur was patchy, his eyes were filled with green goop, his whole body seemed sunken and sad.

*Why does no one want me? The humans. They don't even notice I exist.*

Old Dog laughed. *I could write a book about not being wanted!*

Just then a loud *Clang! Clang! Clang!* sounded and the humans ran out and put Old Dog and Mya Rebecca inside a kennel, banging it shut.

Mya jumped to see what was wrong and the kennel opened. She went out and saw that the gate to the street was wide open too.

Old Dog nudged her from behind. *Kid, get outta here while you can. Before you get sick. Before you go to isolation.*

Mya Rebecca wanted to but she was afraid. *But maybe I'll get adopted!*

Old Dog shook his head. *Kid, listen to me. You have two strikes against you. You're a pit. And you're black. Wish I could go but I'm staying. Too worn out for any adventure.*

Old Dog went back into the kennel, his spindly legs crumbling under him. Mya walked through the gate to the strange street. She looked back at Old Dog and caught his goopy eyes glistening. Then he raised a paw and waved her on.

Mya Rebecca ran and ran and ran. She had no idea where to go, how to find her mom but she just kept running. She ran until she thought her legs would fly off in every direction, or her heart would burst out of her chest. Everything frightened her, the cars whizzing by, the horns honking, the clash of garbage cans. The humans, too. Their long legs and big feet crashing past. No one noticed her, no one cared enough to stop.

Finally Mya Rebecca saw a spread of green as far as she could see. There was grass and trees and no cars. She began walking on a path that went around a lake. She came to what looked like a house, but wasn't, there were no walls. She crawled in and dragged herself to a corner and fell into a heap. She was so tired, hungry and scared. She was so alone. She wanted her mom ... her warm fur and soft tongue, her eyes that followed her everywhere. She wanted to find her, and never leave her again. Mya Rebecca began to cry.

"Hey what's all that caterwauling??"

A tall man sprang up from the side of the house that wasn't a house. Then a bark sounded and out from the dark came a dog. Mya Rebecca stared; the dog was wobbly when it came forward, and she saw he had three legs instead of four.

"Who's this? We have a visitor, Jake!"

The man reached forward and patted Mya's head, then took out from his deep pockets a piece of sandwich, tore it into bites and fed it to her. She gobbled the food down, and he reached back into his coat and got her more. Tripod Dog hobbled over to Mya Rebecca and licked at her mouth.

*You're safe here.* Tripod Dog nodded toward his guardian. *He's the kindest human you'll meet. He has no home like you, but he'll give you all he has ...*

Mya settled into the small space the man and Tripod Dog slept in, her body warmed by theirs. As they snored, Mya looked at the stars above, wondering if her mom was looking up at them, too.

Before the sun rose, Mya got up and carefully left the human and Tripod Dog. She needed to be on her way. She needed to find her mom.

Mya ran through street after street. She soon came to a big fenced in area.
The sound of basketballs rang *clomp clomp clomp* through the air. Kids
were playing, running and laughing. One turned and she saw he had on
eyeglasses so thick his eyes looked like saucers. They were attached in the
back of his head with straps. Then she saw what he was looking at. She
inched over to a beautiful white dog tied to the fence who was watching
every move the boy made.

*Oh, you startled me! I can't hear, you see. Are you lost?*

*I'm looking for my mom.*

Mya hid as the boy walked over to White Dog. He raised his hand and White Dog quickly sat, then laid flat on the ground. The boy stroked her ears and smiled at her, patted his leg and he and White Dog started down the block.

White Dog turned back to Mya. *Good luck finding your mom.*

Mya watched as they left. She thought how wonderful it would be to be loved by a boy like that, and her heart broke.

Mya came to a street with large houses. She hid behind a bush when she heard the strangest *whir whir whir* sound. When she peeked out there was a woman in a big chair, going back and forth on a platform that went from the sidewalk to the porch.

"I'm stuck, Millie! Oh, here we go!"

Behind came a small dog with wheels attached at her middle, her two back legs dangling.

Mya peeked out but she jumped back when the whirring started again.

"Who do we have here, Millie?"

Wheelie Dog came behind Mya Rebecca and sniffed her.

*You're welcome to stay if you like. I can share.*

The woman whirred into the house and came out with a leash that she looped around Mya Rebecca's neck. She led her inside and popped her into a crate that had a bed and blanket in it.

"You can use Millie's crate while you're here. Till we figure out what we're going to do …"

Wheelie Dog went up to the crate and sniffed at her again, put her front paw up on the crate and wheeled away.

The next few days, the woman in the big chair gave Mya a bath and fed her lots of good meals. She brushed her till her coat glistened.

The three of them went for walks, the woman in the big chair and Wheelie Dog and Mya Rebecca on her leash. The woman put up signs on every pole she came to that said "FOUND BEAUTIFUL BLACK PIT PUP ..." but no one ever came or called.

One morning the woman in the big chair took Mya Rebecca to a place with lots of dogs waiting with their guardians. From behind the desk popped the funniest dog Mya had ever seen. He had on sneakers! When he walked his back legs went every which way and his feet made the strangest *skwunch skwunch skwunch* sound. Mya Rebecca stretched her leash as far as it would go so she could get a better look.

*Why do you have on sneakers? Is there something wrong with your legs?*

Sneaker Dog lifted his head up high. *There's nothing wrong with my legs! I was born this way. At least that's what they tell me here all the time. They tell me I'm perfect!*

Mya Rebecca looked around. It wasn't a home. *Do you live here?*

*Yep. Someone tied me to the front door with a note and left me. So I'm what you call a "mascot" now.*

Sneaker Dog winked and *skwunched skwunched* back behind the desk.

Mya Rebecca and the woman in the big chair went in the back and Mya was put on a table. They opened her mouth and squeezed her. They said words like shots and spay. The sights, the sounds, the smells reminded Mya of the scary place and her body tensed and told her to run. When the door opened and the man in the white coat turned, she bolted off the table and out to the hallway.

The woman in the big chair shouted after her and Mya Rebecca could hear the *whir whir whir* of her big chair as she banged against the door again and again to try and get out but Mya didn't stop. She ran and ran, through people's legs and outstretched hands. All she heard in her ears were Old Dog's words ... *kid, get outta here while you can* ... and she did, out the front door and onto the street, around the corner. She didn't stop until she knew no one was following.

For days Mya Rebecca slept behind garbage cans and under benches, curled up tight to keep warm. She ate whatever she could find, pizza crust, a plate of rice and beans.

One morning it was raining and freezing cold. She went down a large set of stairs. A *whoosh* sounded and people rushed in and out of a long silver car. She huddled in a corner against a large pillar.

Mya had never felt so alone and scared. She thought back to all the dogs she had met, Old Dog, Wheelie Dog, Tripod Dog, White Dog and Sneaker Dog. She wanted to be brave like they were, but she didn't feel brave. She wanted the woman in the big chair to rescue her again. She wanted to be back with her mom in the cold backyard. She wanted more than anything to be someplace safe with someone who cared about her.

When Mya woke she was being carried in a man's big arms, then placed in the back seat of a car. Scratchy noises came from the front and they drove really fast. When they brought her inside the building, Mya Rebecca let out a cry.  It was a cry that rose from the bottom of her stomach, pierced through her heart and out her mouth. She howled and howled and howled when she saw where they had brought her. For Mya was back in the scary place, with the cages and the noises and the dogs.

Mya lay huddled in the corner of her cage. She coughed and her head was hot and her body ached. She didn't want to eat. She didn't want to go for walks, or go in the play yard with the other dogs. When the humans walked through, she no longer tried to get them to look at her, to see her. They put a sign on her door that said "kennel cough" and "isolation". She remembered what Old Dog had said about getting sick, about getting out, and she felt in her heart that she might not, and she began to cry softly for herself, for her mom, for all the dogs in the scary place.

The next day the humans who worked there came for her. They slipped the leash around her neck and tugged. She tried to get up but couldn't, her legs were so weak, her chest hurt, she felt so sick. She wanted her mom. She wanted to just go to sleep.

Then she felt something soft on her head and she looked up. A pretty woman had stopped the man and was kneeling down and petting her. Mya got up slowly and moved closer. The woman looked into her eyes and smiled. She was seeing her, Mya Rebecca! The woman motioned to the man holding the leash, and he handed her the card that had been on the front of her cage.

The pretty woman brought her to a big house with pink shutters and put her in a large kennel with a soft comfy bed and a toy and a bone. She gave her pills and chicken stew till she felt much better. Mya had never known the love of a human before and it was the best thing ever, except for one thing. Her mom.

One morning the pretty woman let her go outside. It was the first time she would be with the other dogs in the home. Mya rounded the corner and let out a yell. It was Old Dog! He was with a few others as old and bald and raggedy as he was, lying in the sun on beds. They ran to each other, wagging their tails so hard, their butts wiggled.

*Isn't this the best place ever?*

*I know, kid. Never thought it would happen to an old dog like me but here I am.*

Mya was so happy but sad at the same time. She looked into Old Dog's face and she saw that he understood.

*Still looking for your mom, kid?*

Mya nodded yes and she knew what she had to do. She looked around at the yard and the fence. There was a slat that was loose. She was still a pup and small and she could fit through. She looked at Old Dog and the others, the pretty house with the pink shutters and she felt her eyes fill with tears. But she had to go ...

Mya Rebecca went over to the loose board and began to push her tiny body against it till it gave way, then she flattened down to get under it. She was almost through when she heard the loudest howl, a cry that wasn't sad or angry but something else, something that Mya felt from the tips of her ears to the tips of her paws and she stopped and pulled herself out and looked. She couldn't believe her eyes. She blinked and blinked again. Then she ran in the direction of the howl as fast as her legs had ever carried her. It was her mom! They tumbled around and around and licked and kissed and hugged, both their voices singing with happiness so loud the pretty woman came running out.

"Why, what's this!"

The pretty woman knelt and gathered Mya and her mom up in her arms.

"You two know each other?"

Old Dog and the others came over and sat around them in a circle. The pretty woman glanced from one to the other and Mya knew she was seeing both of them in the same way she had seen Mya in the shelter.

"Well, you're never going to be separated again ..."

Mya and her mom curled up on the pretty woman's lap and all the dogs raised their heads up high and howled with happiness.

For Mya Rebecca, the little black pitbull puppy, was not only finally seen, but loved, as all dogs deserve to be.

### OLD DOG

Inspired by a senior named Jay who was saved from the NY shelter system by REBOUND HOUNDS. Jay spent the remainder of his days with a wonderful hospice family who takes in seniors and gives them a loving home for their final stage in life. www.reboundhounds.org

### TRIPOD DOG

The real Jake was the victim of a horrible car accident. His legs were mutilated; one so badly they had to amputate. He was saved, vetted and rehabbed by IMAGINE PET RESCUE; and later adopted by a loving guardian. Imagine Pet Rescue specializes in medical needs cases, offering a future to injured and sick dogs. www.imaginepetrescue.org

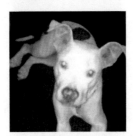

### WHITE DOG

Coco was saved by ALL BREED RESCUE, who did not know at the time she was deaf. They finally found a foster eager to take on a special needs dog, and the foster not only stepped up, but kept her forever!
www.allbreedrescuevt.org

### WHEELIE DOG

Found near death, Millie was saved by UPS 'N DOWNS RESCUE of Connecticut. She had a long, complicated road to recovery, intensive care and spinal surgeries, trips back and forth from NYC to Connecticut. Her last foster home is now her forever, and though Millie loves her "wheelies", through physical therapy, her walking gets better every day!

### SNEAKER DOG

Unable to walk from a severe spinal injury, Ian also suffered from hemophilia. In spite of his condition, RED HOOK DOG RESCUE took on his vetting and rehabilitation, and today Ian is thriving in his home in NYC with two other dogs. Red Hook Dog Rescue is known for their work with special needs dogs and continues to save many from the shelters and streets of NYC.
rhdrdogs@gmail.com

### MYA REBECCA

Originally Rebecca from Brooklyn Animal Care Center, she was saved by REBOUND HOUNDS and later adopted by Sylvia of SCARGO WAGS AND WIGGLES RESCUE in Dennis, MA. This little black pitty girl now knows nothing but love, care and fun provided by her six canine sisters and brothers.
www.scargowagsandwiggles.com

**SHARON AZAR**, Artist. Brooklyn, New York. Born, raised and now living in New York, Sharon first studied with artist, Otto Franz Krone (www.Ottofranzkrone.com). She attended the Art Students League and studied with Professor Sarah Reader at the School of Visual Arts. She has worked on portraits of people and animals, and illustration. She says, "Art has always been for me a way to connect with people and Nature and now that I am retired I can devote more time to art the thing I love most (aside from dogs!)"

Sharon calls her style of art, "paper mosaic", where images are built up via a succession of small pieces of different papers layered and glued together, similar to collage.

**LOREN McAULEY**, Writer. Brooklyn, New York. Loren is a graduate of the MFA Creative Writing Program at NYU. Her short stories have appeared in New Millennium, New York Press, New Rivers Press among others and has been anthologized in American Fiction, Volume 11. She and Karina Strobl are co-founders and partners of Rebound Hounds Rescue.